If Wishes Were Fishes

Retold by **Rose Impey**

Illustrated by *John Eastwood*

ORCHARD BOOKS

Other titles in this series:

Bad Boys and Naughty Girls

Greedy Guts and Belly Busters

I Spy, Pancakes and Pies

Silly Sons and Dozy Daughters

Ugly Dogs and Slimy Frogs

ORCHARD BOOKS
96 Leonard Street, London EC2A 4XD
Orchard Books Australia
14 Mars Road, Lane Cove, NSW 2066
First published in Great Britain in 1999
First paperback edition 2000
Text © Rose Impey 1999
Illustrations © John Eastwood 1999
The right of Rose Impey to be identified as the author
and John Eastwood as the illustrator of this work has been
asserted by them in accordance with the
Copyright, Designs and Patents Act, 1988.
A CIP catalogue record for this book is
available from the British Library.
1 86039 957 6 (hardback)
1 86039 958 4 (paperback)
1 3 5 7 9 10 8 6 4 2 (hardback)
3 5 7 9 10 8 6 4 (paperback)
Printed in Great Britain

★ CONTENTS ★

★ The Three Wishes

We'd all like three wishes. Well, that's what we like to think. But, if wishes were fishes, I bet we'd all throw them back, just like this couple.

One night a man and his wife were sitting in front of their fire, talking, cosy-like. Most of the time they were happy enough, even though they were poor.

But now and again they couldn't help thinking of all the things they would do if they were as rich as their neighbours.

"If only we had a wish," sighed the wife.

"If only we knew a fairy," sighed the man.

And suddenly there was a fairy, right there, in their own kitchen, all shining and smiling at them.

"You can have three wishes,"
said the fairy. "But be careful.
When they've gone, they've gone.
There won't be any more."

And then she disappeared. Puff!
Just like that.

At first the man didn't know
what to say, but his wife did.

"I know what I'll wish for—" she
started to shout.

Quick as a flash, the man
clapped his hand over his wife's
mouth, just in case the fairy was
listening.

"Don't worry," she said, "I'm not wishing yet. But, if I was, I should want to be handsome, rich and famous."

"Handsome, rich and famous!" said the man. "That won't stop you being sick or miserable or dying young. Oh, no. Far better to be hale and healthy and live to a hundred."

"Who'd want to live to a hundred," said the wife, "if you were poor and hungry in the meantime?"

Well, the man couldn't argue with that. Hmmm, he thought. Wishes are as slippery as fishes. "Perhaps we'd better sleep on it," he said.

His wife agreed, "We'll be wiser in the morning than the evening."

But the fire was still burning up brightly, so they sat a little longer, warming their toes and talking, cosy-like.

"It seems a shame to waste this nice fire," said the man.

"Yes," said his wife. "It's a pity, though, we've nothing to cook on it. I wish we had a dozen sausages for our supper."

Uh, oh!
Look what she's done!
She's opened her mouth
And that's one wish gone.

With a sudden whoosh! a long
string of sausages fell down the
chimney, and landed at their feet.

The man was so mad he jumped up out of his chair shouting, "A dozen sausages! What a ninny! What a noodle! What a numskull! I wish the dozen sausages were stuck on the end of your nose, you nincompoop."

Uh, oh!
Look what he's done!
He's opened his mouth
And that's two wishes gone.

The sausages jumped up off the
floor, and stuck on the end of his
wife's nose and hung there like an
elephant's trunk.

"Now what
have you done?"
she cried.

She grabbed hold of the sausages
and tried to pull them off. She
twisted them and turned them. She
pinched them and punched them.
But the sausages wouldn't come
off. Soon she was fizzing mad.

"Don't just stand there," she cried. "Do something, you… gormless galoot."

So then the man tried too.
He pulled and he pulled and he
pulled. The sausages stretched
longer…and longer…and longer.

But when he let go they sprang
back like a piece of elastic and
biffed his wife round the ears –
biff! biff! biff! Then they hung
down, long and floppy again.

"Oh dear, what are we going to do?" said the wife.

"I know just what to do," said her husband. "We must use our last wish to make ourselves rich. Then I shall have a gold case made for you to wear over the sausages."

"A gold case!" His wife couldn't believe her ears.

"And a matching crown," he said. "You'll look very smart."

"Smart?" she screamed. "With a nose as long as a skipping rope! Are you a complete cuckoo? I can't spend the rest of my life with a string of sausages hanging on the end of my nose."

And the poor woman started to sob. Booo-hooo!

It almost made the man laugh to see his wife standing there with tears running down the sausages. But he didn't laugh, for he did truly love her.

"I wish my wife could have her nose back to normal," he said.

Da-daaa!
No sooner said, no sooner done.
He opened his mouth
And the third wish was gone.

Straight away the sausages fell
from her nose. They landed on the
floor and curled themselves up like
a snake.

So, the poor man and his wife didn't get to be rich and famous after all. And who knows whether they lived to a hundred. But I do know one thing: at least they still had the sausages...

"I'll build up the fire," said he.
"I'll put on the pan," said she.
And that's just what they did.
They sat late into the night, frying
sausages and talking, cosy-like.

Hiss! Hiss! Spit! Spat!
It's the end of the story.
That's that!

★ Old Mrs Vinegar ★

There was once an old woman who lived in a vinegar bottle. And do you think she liked it? No, she did not. It was grumble, grumble, grizzle, grizzle, grouch, grouch from morning to night.

One day a fairy was passing
and heard the old woman
grumbling.

"Oh, it's a shame, it's a shame. It is a shame. I shouldn't have to live in a vinegar bottle. I should live in a little cottage, with a thatched roof, and smoke coming out of the chimney, and roses growing round the door. That's where I should live."

The fairy took pity on the old woman. She said to her,

"When you go to bed tonight,
turn three times and close your eyes;
and in the morning
you'll have a surprise."

The old woman did as the fairy said, and, sure enough, she woke next morning and found herself in a little cottage, with a thatched roof, and smoke coming out of the chimney, and roses growing round the door.

Well, wasn't she surprised! And wasn't she pleased! But she quite forgot to thank the fairy.

Now, this fairy was a busy one.
She flew north, she flew south, she
flew east and she flew west, on her
fairy business.

After a while, she said to herself, "I wonder how the old woman is getting on? She must be very happy in her own little house."

But she wasn't. The old woman was grumbling and grizzling again.

"Oh, it's a shame, it's a shame. It is a shame," she said. "I shouldn't have to live in this poky little cottage, all on my own.
I should live in a smart new house, with lace curtains and a brass door-knocker, in a street with lots of nice neighbours. That's where I should live."

The fairy was surprised and a little sad. But she said to the old woman,

"When you go to bed tonight,
turn three times and close your eyes;
and in the morning
you'll have a surprise."

The old woman did as the fairy said, and next morning she woke and found herself in a smart new house, with lace curtains and a brass door-knocker, in a street with lots of nice neighbours.

The old woman was surprised.
And she was certainly pleased. But
she still forgot to thank the fairy.

The fairy was as busy as ever: she flew north, she flew south, she flew east and she flew west, on her fairy business.

After a while she said to herself, "I'll go and see how the old woman's getting on. I'm sure she'll be happy now, in her smart new house."

But was she happy? I don't think so.

"Oh, it's a shame, it's a shame. It is a shame," she grumbled. "I shouldn't have to live in a street with all the houses the same, and common people each side of me. I should live in a mansion in the country, with gardens all round it and servants to come when I ring a bell. That's where I should live."

The fairy was disappointed and rather cross. But she said to the old woman,

"When you go to bed tonight,
turn three times and close your eyes;
and in the morning
you'll have a surprise."

Just as the fairy said, when the old woman woke next morning she found herself in a mansion in the country, with gardens all round it, and servants to come when she rang a bell.

Pleased? She was delighted. But do you think she remembered to thank the fairy? No, I don't think so, either.

Our fairy was flying north, flying south, flying east, flying west; as busy as ever on her fairy business.

But she still remembered the old woman. "She must be happy now," thought the fairy, "in her mansion in the country."

But not a bit of it! The old woman was at it again.

"Oh, it's
a shame,
it's a shame.
It is a shame.
I shouldn't
have to live here in
the middle of nowhere,
with no one to talk to.
I should be a duchess,
with a coach and horses,
and footmen running beside me,
off to visit the queen."

Our fairy didn't like the sound
of that, I can tell you. But she
said,

"When you go to bed tonight,
turn three times and close your eyes;
and in the morning
you'll have a suprise."

Well, when the old woman woke next morning there she was, a duchess with a coach and horses and footmen running beside her, off to visit the queen. She was far too busy to thank the fairy.

The fairy was busy too. Busy, busy, busy, north, south, east and west on her fairy business. When she did stop, the first thing she thought of was the old woman.

"Surely she's happy now that she's a duchess," she said to herself.

But what did she find? The old
woman, dressed in silks and satins,
waiting at the door for her,
looking as cross as ever.

"It is such a shame," she said, in a very grand voice, "that I should have to bow and curtsey to the queen. I should like to be a queen. I should like to sit on a golden throne and have everyone curtsey to me. That's what I should like."

The fairy was very sad and very, very cross. But she didn't lose her temper. She said quite quietly, "Very well. When you go to bed tonight..."

"Yes, yes, yes," snapped the old woman. "I know what to do."

So the fairy flew away.

The old woman sighed and
grumbled about having to wait
until bedtime. But at last it came
and she went upstairs. She turned
three times and closed her eyes.
And in the morning…what a
surprise!

There she was back in her old vinegar bottle. And she may still be there, for all I know.

So, back she went
to where she began.
Now, tell me a better one,
if you can.

The Three Wishes is a very old story found in many languages. This version is based on the French story by Madame de Beaumont. *Old Mrs Vinegar* is a simpler and shorter version of *The Fisherman and his Wife*, one of Grimm's Fairy Tales.

Here are some more stories you might like to read:

About Wishes:

The Demon and the Jug
from *The Illustrated Book of Fairy Tales*
by Neil Philip
(Dorling Kindersley)

The Fisherman and his Wife
from *Classic Fairy Tales to Read Aloud*
selected by Naomi Lewis
(Kingfisher)

About Another Grumbler:

The Discontented Fish
from *African Myths and Legends*
by Kathleen Arnott
(Oxford)